Three Together

igloo

igloo

This edition published in 2008
by Igloo Books Ltd
Cottage Farm,
Sywell,
NN6 0BJ
www.igloo-books.com

10 9 8 7 6 5 4 3 2 1

ISBN: 978 1 84561 928 2

Cover design by Insight Design
Cover illustrated by © Rachel Ellen Designs Ltd
Interior illustrations by Liz and Kate Pope

Printed and manufactured in China

The Mystery
of the
Rainbow Necklace

by Carol Lawrence

igloo

Chapter 1

A Splash and a Dash

"Race you to the water!" Poppy called to her best friend, KC.

They ran into the sparkling sea, giggling. It was sunny, the sand was warm and the two friends were having the best time ever on the beach.

Aunt Kathryn, watching on the shore, and Sam, Poppy's seven-and-a-half year old brother – away from the computer for once – were trying to make a giant spaceship out of sand. But Poppy and KC were having much more fun in the water. They pushed their brightly coloured bodyboards a little further out and waited for a wave to come along, so they could try to ride it.

Poppy blew her black hair out of her bright green eyes and looked for KC. She was lying on the board and waiting, just as Poppy was. Here came the wave! It rose up under Poppy and carried her almost all the way back to the beach.

"Bleurgh!" called out KC, behind her. "I fell off again."

"Don't worry, KC," Poppy shouted back, watching her best friend laughing and splashing in the water. "We'll get the hang of it soon!"

Poppy and KC did everything together. KC knew all of Poppy's secrets, and Poppy knew all of KC's . . . except what the letters in KC's name really stood for! KC wouldn't tell anyone. Poppy thought it was very cool to have a best friend with such a good secret.

Just as Poppy was about to get back on her bodyboard, she heard a sploshing sound next to her. Turning to see what it was, she saw something small, something that glinted red, yellow, green, purple - all the colours of the rainbow - fall into the water. Whatever it was, it was already sinking!

"What's that?" asked KC, paddling up.

"I don't know," answered Poppy. "But I'm going to find out." She held her breath and dove under the surface. She saw the coloured object being pulled away by the tide. Quickly, she grabbed it and lifted it to the surface.

It was a necklace with sparkling stones - a different coloured stone for each colour of the rainbow.

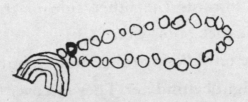

"It's beautiful!" breathed KC, splashing over. "How did it get here?"

Poppy turned to look across the beach. It was almost deserted, apart from Sam and Aunt Kathryn. Or was it? If she squinted, Poppy could see someone walking quickly away from the sea, a little way off. Someone who was pulling a hood up over their head, even though it was so warm. The sun was in Poppy and KC's eyes, so they couldn't tell if it was a boy or a girl.

"Hello!" Poppy called across the water. "You dropped your necklace!"

The figure stopped. But instead of turning round, it suddenly began to run. But, instead of running back towards Poppy and KC, whoever it was, was running away!

Poppy splashed out of the water as fast as she could and ran towards the strange figure. It was heading towards the other side of the beach, where the rock pools were.

"Come on!" Poppy called to KC, but KC was already right behind her. They ran over the sand, but with the sun in their eyes it was hard to see where they were going. Poppy had to scrunch up her eyes to see the person ahead. They were moving fast!

By the time Poppy and KC reached the rock pools, they could see that the mysterious figure was clambering over the rocks at top speed. "I wish we had our shoes," KC sighed. "Now we've got to climb all over those spiky rocks!"

"Do you want to give up?" panted Poppy.

"No way!" grinned KC, and they set off over the boulders.

It wasn't easy. Some of the rocks were covered in slimy seaweed, and others were clustered with barnacles that made their feet hurt. Poppy stepped in a rock pool, and saw a little crab scuttle away. The friends clambered over the rocks as fast as they could, but the person they were chasing was getting further and further away. As KC caught up with Poppy, they both saw that the running figure had climbed up the low rocks by the edge of the beach. The rocks led back onto Seaview Street, the lane that ran by the edge of the beach. The street was filled with souvenir shops and people eating ice cream. And, without shoes, there was no way Poppy and KC could climb up!

The two friends rested on the rocks for a moment, panting. "I guess whoever it was really didn't want their necklace back!" huffed Poppy. She looked at the necklace carefully for the first time. It was really pretty. Each stone was almost transparent. But Poppy realized that the chain was broken. One piece of the chain had been broken, and the necklace wouldn't join together to make a loop any more.

"Wait for me!" panted Sam as he climbed over the rocks, his face red with effort. He hated it when he was left behind. "Why did you run off like that? Aunt Kathryn was worried!"

Poppy explained what had happened, and showed him the necklace. "Why would someone throw this in the water?" she asked. "And then run away?"

"Whatever," snorted Sam. It was his favourite word. "There has to be a reason. There's a reason for everything!"

"Maybe they didn't want it any more because it was broken," wondered KC.

"But then why would they run off?" asked Poppy. "A broken necklace isn't very scary, and neither are we!" She thought hard for a moment. Poppy was good at thinking hard. Sometimes, when she thought particularly hard, she came up with ideas that nobody else had thought of. She looked around her, wishing that this could be one of those times. All she could see was rocks and sand, stretching out to the sea. But what was that mark over there?

"Wait! Don't move!" Poppy said. "I can see something."

Sam and KC looked at her in confusion. "What?" asked KC.

"I've thought of a way to find out who this necklace belongs to," said Poppy. She pointed between two large, barnacle-covered rocks. "Don't walk on that piece of sand!" Poppy climbed over to it. "Look," she said, and KC and Sam craned their heads over.

It was a footprint in the fine white sand, still slightly damp. It must have been made by a sneaker. There was a lightning symbol in the middle of it.

"I know that logo," said Sam. "Wow, he was wearing a pair of

AirWave 3000s! They're super-cool shoes. No wonder he went so fast!"

"We couldn't see if it was a boy or a girl," KC reminded him. "It could be either."

Poppy saw that Sam had his new camera around his neck. "Take a picture, Sam!" she said. "This is a really important clue."

Sam snapped the shoe-print and they walked back across the rocks, a lot more slowly this time. The sun was starting to dip in the sky, the shadows were getting longer, and the sea was turning from a brilliant blue to a deep, mysterious green. "Just like the necklace," thought Poppy as they stepped back onto the sand. Except that had red and orange and purple and all the colours of the rainbow.

Aunt Kathryn was standing with all their beach gear, waving at them to come over. They knew she wouldn't be angry at them, though. She was too cool for that. In fact, Aunt Kathryn was just about Poppy's favourite grown-up, apart from Mum and Dad. Aunt Kathryn lived by the sea and did a ton of cool, outdoor things. Things like windsurfing and volleyball and rollerskating and anything she wanted, as long as it was fun and fast and lively. Poppy, KC and Sam were staying with Aunt Kathryn for the whole week, while their parents were away. They still had six days to go. Six whole days of beach fun!

When they reached Aunt Kathryn, they showed her the necklace and told them about the strange chase. "It happened so fast," Poppy thought, "that it already seems as if it happened to someone else." It was the kind of thing you saw on TV or read about in a book. Not something that happened in real life.

"Weird," said Aunt Kathryn. Some grown-ups would have added something boring like "Better forget about it," or "It's not important," or even "Give me the necklace to take care of. That would have been awful."

But Aunt Kathryn just said, "It's a mystery. And you three are going to have to solve it!"

The three friends smiled at her. Aunt Kathryn knew they all loved mysteries and, most of all, loved solving them. "Sam, you should check your photo of the shoe print on the computer at home. Come on, everyone!"

"We have a rainbow necklace, a mysterious person to find and a clue to find them with," said Poppy, looking at the sea again and running ahead. "Let's go!"

Chapter 2

Josh and Huxley

The next day, the friends didn't have a lot of time to think about the necklace straight away. Aunt Kathryn had promised to take them on a boat trip around the bay. They went down to the boat, moored in the little marina. It was a big, white, shiny one called Marlin, and it sparkled almost as much as the sea itself. Poppy, KC and Sam knew they'd have a great trip, because Aunt Kathryn was friends with the man who owned it.

They jumped on board and the captain came to shake hands. He was a tall, smiling man with fair hair and a tanned face. "Hello, you three," He said, smiling. "I'm Kevin."

"Hi, Captain Kevin!" said Poppy. "I thought captains of boats were meant to be old and have white beards and smoke pipes and wear big sweaters with anchors on them!"

Captain Kevin laughed. "Maybe one day I'll have a big beard - but I think I'd collapse in this heat if I wore a big sweater!" He took them to the side of the boat and showed them the view. It was another beautiful day, and the seagulls were gliding over the sky above the calm waves.

"This is Joshua," Captain Kevin said, pointing to a skinny boy hanging by his arms from a rail that stretched over the deck. His feet didn't reach to the ground, and he was swinging happily.

"Hi," said Joshua, without letting go of the rail, as if he hung there all the time. "Dad, where's Huxley?"

"Huxley! Here, boy!" called Captain Kevin, and suddenly a big, funny, furry dog rushed up to the friends from the gangplank. He was white and grey and shaggy, and he had hair coming down right in front of his eyes. His tongue hung out and his big, floppy tail was wagging furiously. Poppy and Sam were delighted! They'd left their dog Jasper at home, along with KC's cat, Millie. It was great to meet a new doggy friend.

Joshua let go of the rail and landed on the deck with a thump. "Huxley!" he shouted, looking overjoyed. "He's my dog, and he's the best one there is!" He grabbed Huxley and rolled around the deck with him, while Huxley panted and woofed and gave a big doggy grin.

KC was a little frightened at first. She didn't like dogs much, especially if they barked loudly or growled. But Huxley didn't seem to be a growly sort of dog. He was so happy and cute - even though he was so big - that soon she was patting his head and hugging him, just like Poppy and Sam were already doing.

Josh seemed happy they were there. "You have to come exploring with me," he said. "I know all the best places in town, and all around the bay. We can go fossil hunting, or look for shipwrecks, or anything you like." Poppy, KC and Sam all agreed.

"That sounds great, Josh," said Poppy. "Does Huxley come with you too?"

"Just try to keep him away!" beamed Josh. "He goes everywhere I go. Sometimes he's even better at exploring than I am!"

Other people were already joining the boat for the trip around the bay. Poppy, KC and Sam recognised some of them. They were all people who stayed at the hotels on Seaview Street, or in the small houses by the beach. One girl, Megan, was from Poppy's school. She waved when she saw the friends.

"Poppy!" said Megan, breathlessly. "How are you, and you, and you, and are you having a good time, and have you been to the shops, and on the beach, and did you put enough lotion on, because it's a very hot day?" Megan always talked like that. If you wanted to talk with Megan, you had to make sure you weren't in a hurry, because she could talk forever.

Another group of grown-ups came aboard,

with a thin, older girl in a sleeveless t-shirt. Seeing all these people gave Poppy an idea. "Let's ask them all if they know anything about the rainbow necklace," she suggested to KC and Sam.

But, before they could answer, they all felt a lurch underfoot. "The boat has set sail!" exclaimed KC.

"Don't be silly," said Sam. "This boat doesn't have a sail. It's got a motor."

"Oh, Sam," groaned KC. "You know what I mean!"

"Whatever!"

The boat was moving slowly out of the marina. Before long, they could see the whole of the bay laid out in front of them; colourful Seaview Street, the long pier, the sandy beach

and the rock pools next to it, all baking in the sun.

"That's Falcon Point," said Megan, pointing to a rocky cliff rising above a pebbly part of the beach. "You get a great view from up there. I know because my mum and my brother and my sister and my other brother and my dad and my dad's friend and I went up there . . . " Megan talked happily, and didn't seem to notice that the others were smiling, waiting for her to stop.

"We'll be back in a while," said Poppy, dragging the others off. She wanted to speak to everyone about the necklace. After all, any of these people could be the owner.

She decided to start with the older girl in the t-shirt, even though she looked a little bit frightening. Poppy tried to make herself feel brave. Most people, she told herself, are nice when you get to know them. She walked over to where the girl was gazing out to sea.

When she saw Poppy, she scowled. "What do you want?" said the girl.

"Um," said Poppy, feeling all her courage melt

away. "I found this, um, necklace yesterday. Is it yours?" She held it out for the girl to see. But the girl's face was blank.

"Never seen it before, wouldn't want it. Cheap. Only a little girl would wear this. Is that all?"

"Um . . . yes," said Poppy in a small voice, and walked away. "Okay," she thought. "So maybe all people aren't nice when you speak to them."

KC had seen what happened. "Don't worry," she said, squeezing Poppy's arm. "You were so brave to go and talk to her. I could never have done that."

Just hearing KC say that made Poppy feel a lot better. KC always knew the right thing to say.

"Oh, don't worry about her," interrupted Josh, as he dashed past with Huxley. "That's Tyler. Tyler Jackson. Spends most of her time in a little shack on the edge of the beach. Nobody knows what she does there. She might be a spy, or a . . . a witch!"

The girls looked at him in surprise. "Well, you never know!" he added, ruffling Huxley's hair and looking embarrassed.

Chapter 3

Two Little Letters

As the morning wore on, Poppy, KC and Sam went around the boat, asking almost everyone about the necklace. Nobody seemed to know anything, but at least they all seemed nicer than Tyler. Tyler didn't talk to anyone at all, and nobody seemed interested in talking to her, either.

Eventually, Poppy, KC and Sam took a break and sat looking at the shimmering water. Poppy held the necklace up and watched the stones sparkle in the light, casting beautiful rainbow shadows onto the white sides of the boat. One of the sections turned slowly, and she thought she saw something marked on it. Looking at it closely, she checked it again. Something was scratched neatly into the red stone. It was just two letters: I.C.

"Look at this!" Poppy said in astonishment. "Another clue!"

"Those are probably the initials of someone's name," said Sam.

"Someone who owns the necklace," added KC.

Poppy went straight to Aunt Kathryn, who was talking to another grown-up about skateboarding. "Do you know anyone here with the initials I.C.?" she asked. "There must be someone!"

"I.C. . . . I.C . . . No, I don't think so," mused Aunt Kathryn. "It's a very good clue, though."

It wasn't long before Poppy, KC and Sam had told everyone about the initials. Megan was very excited when she heard. "I know someone! I know! I'll go and get her!" Megan rushed inside the boat and came out holding the hand of a pretty-looking woman in a white dress. "This is my mum's friend, Imogen! And her second name's Clear! Imogen Clear, I. C.!"

"Excuse me," Poppy said, "But is this your necklace?"

The woman took the necklace, looked at it and smiled in a puzzled way. "No, I'm sorry," she said. "I've never seen this before. But good luck with your detecting!"

Poppy sighed. It was so unfair, to find someone with the right initials, and not to find the necklace's owner!

She must have looked a little annoyed, because Aunt Kathryn called Poppy, KC and Sam over. "I wasn't going to tell you this until later, but you look like you need cheering up!" she said. "On your last day here, we're going to have a party on the beach. How would you like that?"

"Oh, wow!" said Poppy, KC and Sam together. The necklace was forgotten, at least for a moment.

"Can we have a barbecue?" asked Sam.

"And party games? And sports and competitions?" said Poppy.

KC didn't say anything, though. Aunt Kathryn wasn't her aunt, after all. It seemed rude for her to make demands to a grown-up.

"Yes, those are good ideas," said Aunt Kathryn. "And you can invite anyone you like!"

Aunt Kathryn could see that KC was holding back. "What would you like at the party, KC?" she asked.

"Um . . . could we have dancing?" KC asked, a little shyly.

Aunt Kathryn smiled. "Of course we can, sweetheart. And you can choose the music, too!" KC smiled back at her.

Poppy and KC loved parties. They started talking excitedly about what they would do and how they would help organise it. They were just working out what cakes they ought to have when, out of nowhere, a thought about the necklace popped into Poppy's head.

"KC," she said thoughtfully, "the necklace was thrown in the water, right?"

"Yes?" said KC.

"Well, what if the person who threw it wanted

to get rid of it because they stole it?" Poppy said excitedly. "Maybe they were worried they were going to get caught, so they threw it in the sea! That way, nobody would ever know it was them!"

The three friends thought about it. "Right," said Sam. "When we saw them, they thought we would realise they'd taken it from someone. So they ran away!"

"But who would steal a necklace?" asked KC. "I mean, everyone seems so nice around here. There's nobody who would do that . . ." Even as KC spoke, someone moved away from the deck, and they saw Tyler, the bad-tempered girl, scowling at the water.

They looked at each other. "You don't think it could be her?" asked Poppy.

Sam shrugged. "I don't know," he said. "She seems so grouchy."

KC frowned. "Maybe she's just shy."

Tyler turned her head and saw them watching. She gave them a haughty look and turned back to the water.

"I don't know, either," said Poppy. "But it's worth checking out!"

When they got off the boat at lunchtime, the three friends couldn't stop talking about Tyler. "We need to find out if she has a pair of those shoes," said Poppy. "What were they called, Sam?"

"AirWave 3000s. Super-cool," said Sam.

"That would show she could have made that shoe print!" Poppy explained.

KC nodded. "So how do we find out? Do we go and ask her?"

Poppy remembered how rude Tyler had been. "I don't want to talk to her again," she said. "Even if she does have those shoes, she might not tell us anyway."

"What did Josh say?" wondered KC. "Tyler has a shack down by the beach, right?"

The three friends looked at one another. Poppy was the first to say it. "We should go down there and investigate." Poppy liked the sound of that: investigate. It somehow made the hunt for the rainbow necklace owner seem a lot more important and exciting.

After lunch, they went back down to the beach and watched for Tyler. Soon enough, she came striding past, not even looking in their direction. She walked past several of the small huts on the beach, until she came to one that looked particularly dark, dingy and depressing. She went straight in, slamming the door behind her.

Aunt Kathryn waved at them from the other side of the beach. "Come on, guys!" she called. "The movie will be starting soon!" Aunt Kathryn had promised to take them to the movies that afternoon.

"Let's come back tomorrow," said Poppy. "I guess it's okay if we just take a peek inside."

The sun was already setting when they returned to Aunt Kathryn's little house after watching the movie. The house wasn't far from the beach, and was full of sports gear, surfboards and big posters of rock bands. Poppy and KC had a room all to themselves, and Sam had a sleeping bag on the couch.

After they had brushed their teeth that night and were ready for bed, Sam stayed up for a while. He was sitting at the computer, finding pictures of AirWave 3000s.

"Here they are," he called, and Poppy and KC came to look. It was a picture of silver shoes, with blue stripes running up the sides in a lightning pattern. "If we can find someone with these shoes, maybe they'll be the person who had the necklace."

Sam and KC talked some more about the next day, and whether they'd be brave enough to look into Tyler's shack.

But Poppy was quiet, thinking hard. "What if Tyler was telling the truth?" she said to herself. "Maybe she really hasn't seen the rainbow necklace before. After all, there are lots of other people around the beach every day."

Poppy couldn't help thinking about the

necklace as she said goodnight to Aunt Kathryn and got into bed. "Someone out there must be missing the necklace," she thought. "If Sam was right, the necklace might even have been stolen from them!" Before she drifted off to sleep, Poppy made a decision. She was going to find out who the rainbow necklace belonged to . . . no matter what.

Chapter 4
The Surprise in the Shack

The next morning, Poppy, KC and Sam took their beach things and made their way to the small shacks. They were a short walk away from the beach, and hardly anybody seemed to be coming in or out of the shacks. They were mostly used by people who hired them for the day while they were on the beach. It looked like most of the shacks were empty now.

"Come on," whispered Poppy, even though they were outside and nobody could hear them. "Let's investigate!"

They crept up to the shack that they had seen Tyler go into the day before. Standing on tiptoes, Poppy peered through the window. The glass was grimy and the inside of the shack was dark. She could

hardly see anything at all. Eventually, she made out some odd shapes in the gloom. What was that tall, strange coloured shape? And was that someone standing there? "No," Poppy thought. "It must be a dummy or something, because it doesn't move." She swallowed and turned to KC and Sam. "There's no one inside," she said. "We're going in."

Poppy knew that if she waited any longer, she'd get even more nervous. She pushed open the door of the shack. It creaked open, and Poppy stepped inside.At first, she couldn't see very much at all. It was too dark after the sunlight outside. Everything seemed musty and dusty, and there was a smell of paint and sawdust. KC and Sam stepped in nervously right behind her.

"Maybe we should wait until Tyler's here," whispered KC.

"Close the door, Sam," said Poppy, trying to sound braver than she felt. "That way, nobody will know we're in here." As her eyes got used to the dark, she saw what was filling the little shack. Propped up on easels, hanging on the walls, resting against the dusty desk, were paintings. Paintings of ships at sea, rainbows breaking through clouds, children  playing on the sand. In fact, anything happy and colourful that you could think of.

"Do you think Tyler painted all this?" Poppy wondered.

For a while, the three children just stared. There were also models hanging from the ceiling: boats made out of wood, paper-maché beach balls and bright white seagulls. The person-shaped figure that Poppy had seen outside wasn't a dummy; it was a big paper-maché model of a multi-coloured, smiling man.

"Wow," said KC.

Sam was busy staring at the models on the ceiling. "They must have taken ages to make!" he said.

Poppy remembered what they had come in here for. "We're meant to be looking for clues," Poppy reminded Sam and KC. "Sam, you check around the floor. I'll look on the desk and, KC, you can . . . " She stopped. The door of the shack was creaking, and even before Poppy could turn around, someone had stepped inside.

It was Tyler! The three friends were so surprised, they couldn't speak. Would Tyler shout at them? Throw them out? Tell Aunt Kathryn that they'd been caught trespassing? But, instead, Tyler gave a small smile. A very small smile but, still, it was a smile.

"Have you been looking around?"

"Um . . . yes," said Poppy, confused.

"That's why I leave the door unlocked," said Tyler, striding past them and filling a jam jar with water from the dirty sink. "People can come in and see all this stuff any time. If they want." She shrugged.

"We like, the, um . . . " Sam started, but KC interrupted.

"It's amazing! Did you really do it all? The pictures of the beach? And the models? And the big man?"

Tyler was already sorting through some brushes on her desk. "Yeah. I guess. Some people say it's okay."

Tyler didn't turn around.

Poppy wasn't just good at spotting clues. She was pretty good at noticing things about people, too. Looking at the way Tyler acted, Poppy thought she could see what Tyler was really like. "Tyler must be really shy!" thought Poppy. "She pretends to be gruff and grizzly because she worries about what people will think of her. I bet whenever she's outside or at school, she'd rather be in here, painting." Poppy smiled, but Tyler didn't see. Instead, Tyler said, "If you've seen everything, you'd better go."

The friends looked at each other. They didn't want to go, not just yet. Poppy said, "You know, we're not in a hurry or anything."

Tyler turned around and looked at them properly for the first time.

"I mean, if you didn't mind us hanging around, we could sort of . . . stay and watch you, if that's OK," Poppy suggested.

That tiny smile reappeared on Tyler's face. She shrugged. "Don't mind," she said, and turned back to her painting.

So Poppy, Sam and KC watched quietly as Tyler mixed some paints and started daubing them on a big canvas. At first, Tyler didn't say anything to them but, as she relaxed and became more and more involved in her painting, she started talking.

"You know those seagulls that were flying over the boat yesterday? I had an idea about how I could do them with silver paint, maybe put some foil down for the water . . . probably a stupid idea."

"No," said KC eagerly, "it sounds awesome. What are those pretty stones on the desk?"

"They're for a mosaic," said Tyler. "You know, a big picture made out of bits of glass and stones and stuff?"

KC's eyes shone. "Yes," she said. "Are you making one?"

"I don't have enough to start it yet," said Tyler,

"But when I do it'll be amazing - I mean, it could be, probably won't, though. . ." She folded her arms and looked a bit annoyed with herself for being so excited about it.

Poppy could see that KC wanted to ask if she could join in with the painting. She nudged her. "Go on, KC! I bet Tyler would love for you to help!"

But KC shook her head, wide-eyed. "No," she whispered. "She wouldn't like it." And, although they stayed for a little while longer, KC wouldn't say anything about helping Tyler. Sam carefully picked up the models and Tyler told him how they were made. Poppy wandered around the little shack, looking at the paintings. She didn't want to look for clues about the rainbow necklace just now – it didn't seem right, somehow. But she knew she had to keep trying. She went up to Tyler, who was laying down a thick coat of green paint for the sea on her painting.

"We're still trying to find out who this necklace belongs to," said Poppy. "I guess you already said you didn't know anything, though." She took the necklace out of her backpack. Tyler took it, and looked at it much more closely than she had on the boat.

"No, sorry," she said, shaking her head. She held it up to the light and watched the colours. "I guess it is pretty nice, though," she said quietly, not looking at Poppy. "I'm sorry I said it wasn't. Hey, it's broken. Do you want me to fix it?"

"Would you really? I mean, could you?" asked Poppy excitedly. "That'd be great!"

"No problem," said Tyler. "Easy. I'll do it tomorrow, first thing." Poppy gave Tyler the necklace, and she put it in on the desk. "Don't worry," she said, "I'll take good care of it." Tyler seemed a little bit embarrassed at offering to help. "It's no big deal."

KC interrupted. "Who's outside? I thought I heard someone. Maybe it's someone else who wants to see your paintings?"

Poppy opened the door and looked around, but there was nobody there. "Whoever it was, they're gone now."

Tyler sucked the end of her paintbrush thoughtfully. "There is something you could do that might help you," she said. "I'm pretty sure they sell that kind of necklace in town. You could go around the shops and ask if they've sold one lately."

"That's a great idea, Tyler!" said Poppy. Suddenly, she was full of energy again. "What do you say?" she asked, turning to KC and Sam. "Are you ready for some window shopping tomorrow?"

Sam and KC agreed. It wasn't quite a clue, but it was almost as good!

Chapter 5

Shopping for Clues

Poppy, KC and Sam enjoyed that afternoon. They stayed with Tyler in the shack for a while longer, and then wandered back onto the beach. Poppy and KC practiced on their bodyboards while Sam looked for crabs in the nearest rock pools. They were surprised to find how tired they were when it was finally time to leave the beach for dinner and bed.

The next day, Poppy, KC and Sam went down to Seaview Street. It was full of people busy shopping, chatting and enjoying the sun. A few clouds floated across the sun from time to time, but they didn't spoil anyone's mood.

"It's a good day to go detecting in town," said Poppy, and KC and Sam agreed. There were lots of small shops down Seaview Street, selling everything from chocolate to ice cream to souvenirs. The three friends had decided to spend the morning hunting around the shops to see if they could find any that sold the necklace, and then drop in on Tyler again in the afternoon. Aunt Kathryn was clothes shopping, and the friends had been allowed to do their own shopping for a while before meeting up again.

"Poppy," said Sam, looking around him, "Do we have to go into all these shops?"

"Yes," said Poppy.

"Even the ones with all the toys in the window? And the ones that sell twenty different types of ice cream?"

"I guess we do, if we're going to find out about the necklace," said Poppy.

Sam punched the air. "YESSS!" he said. "This is my perfect day!"

KC and Poppy laughed. "Let's start with this one - it's got robots!" said Sam, dragging Poppy into a nearby shop. It was time to do some serious browsing!

Ten shops later, the three friends still hadn't found anywhere that sold the exact same necklace as the one in Poppy's pocket. Even Sam was beginning to get a bit bored by all the shops, which mostly seemed to sell the same things, anyway. "When you've seen one water-squirting plastic dolphin," he said sadly, "you've seen them all." The friends ambled down the street, trying not to think about all the ice cream they'd seen. Their stomachs were rumbling, and it was nearly lunchtime.

Sam saw a brightly-painted shop and ran towards it. "Let's go in this one! This is bound to have necklaces!" The little shop had windows full of all kinds of chocolate, but no jewellery at all.

Poppy looked at KC and sighed. "Not much chance here." Still, they pushed the door open and went inside.

On one side, there were a few necklaces hanging up on a rotating display. Sam was pointing at them and looking rather smug. "See?" he said. "I'm always right!"

♡ ☆ ♡ ☆ ♡

As they looked at them, the shopkeeper moved down the counter to talk to them. "Looking for a necklace? We're almost out, I'm afraid," he said, looking out at them from under bushy eyebrows.

"Oh, it was just one special one, but I don't think it's here," said Poppy. "One that was all the colours of the rainbow."

The shopkeeper blinked. "We sold the last one a few days ago," he said, sounding apologetic.

"Did you?" Poppy asked. "With sparkling stones? And a silvery chain?"

"I'm afraid so," said the shopkeeper. "A little girl bought it. She was very excited."

Sam tapped her on the shoulder. "Poppy, even if it was the right sort of necklace, and even if someone bought it a few days ago, that doesn't mean it's our necklace."

Poppy looked downcast. "Yeah. I know. You're right, Sam."

"Funnily enough," said the shopkeeper, scratching his head, "I remember, because she said she was going to scratch her initials in it."

KC and Poppy hugged each other, and Sam

punched the air again. The shopkeeper was very surprised.

"It must be her. She must be I.C.! Sir, we found her necklace and we want to give it back," said Poppy, in a rush. "Could you tell us what she looked like? Did she say her name?"

"Oh," mused the shopkeeper, "She was just . . . a normal little girl, really. Don't know her name. She had brown hair and pigtails, I think. I'm sorry. I can't be more help."

Still, it was a real and definite and actual clue, the first one they'd found since the shoe print in the sand. The shopkeeper watched as the kids danced out of the shop. "Well, it's nice to make people happy," he said, and went back to polishing his counter. "Even if I don't know what I said to do it!"

Chapter 6

Mess and Stress

Poppy, KC and Sam couldn't help talking all the way through lunch at Aunt Kathryn's house. "We know what she looks like!" said KC.

"We know what shoes she wore!" said Poppy.

"We know she's called I.C.!" said Sam.

Aunt Kathryn laughed. "At this rate, you'll soon know what toothpaste she uses and what she likes for breakfast."

"We'll probably work that out next," said Poppy, clearing her plate in extra-quick time. "Now, we just need to find her!"

The friends were in a great mood as they hurried down to the beach to tell Tyler the good news. Now they'd made friends with her, they

felt sure she would be glad they'd found such an important clue.

They weren't expecting to see Tyler sitting outside the shack, her head in her hands. Poppy ran up to her.

"Tyler? What's the matter? Has something happened?"

Tyler hardly looked up. She just pointed inside the shack. Poppy looked inside. Oh, no!

Paintings were knocked over, some of the models were on the floor, and paint was splashed everywhere. What on earth had happened?

"It was like this when I got here," said Tyler, miserably. "I spent so much time on these, and now someone's messed it all up, and I don't know what to do!"

Poppy sat down next to Tyler and put her arm around her. "Don't worry," she said. "We'll help you clean it up."

"Yes," said KC, "Maybe it was an accident. Maybe someone came in and knocked something over."

"We'll help!" said Sam. "It's not so bad, really!"

Tyler looked at them gratefully. "Thank you. Are you sure? I don't need you to - I mean it would be really nice if you did, but you don't have to." But the three had already gone into the shack and started cleaning.

Sam was right: it wasn't quite as bad as it looked. Although there was paint all over the floor, most of it was from just one pot of purple paint. None of the paintings was damaged, apart from a few spots of paint, and 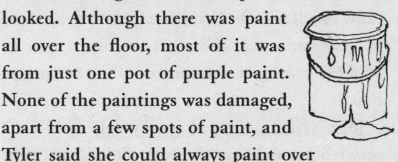 Tyler said she could always paint over those. Just as it was looking as though the four of them would be able to sort it all out, there was a knock on the door.

"Come in," said Tyler, who was feeling a lot better. She was scrubbing at one of the last bits of purple paint.

It was Josh and his dad, Captain Kevin. But they both looked very unhappy. Josh stood in the doorway. "Josh, are you all right?" asked Poppy.

"You look like you're sick."

Josh was very pale. "I came to say sorry," he said quickly. "Sorry for ruining your paintings."

"Josh?" said Tyler, hugging herself, as if it had suddenly just got cold. "You did this? Why?"

But Josh just scowled and wouldn't say a word.

Captain Kevin looked at him angrily. "Josh came to tell me what he'd done. He says he came in here and made this mess. But he won't say why. He's being very stupid and I'm ashamed of him."

Josh went from looking very pale to looking very red. He stared at the floor, and seemed to be muttering something under his breath. "Sorry," he eventually said again.

"He's going to be grounded for a week," added Captain Kevin. "Which means he won't be able to go to your party, I'm afraid," he said to Poppy, Sam and KC.

Now it was the friends' turn to feel sad. They didn't want Josh to have to miss out on the fun, even if he had been so stupid.

Poppy could see that Tyler didn't know what to say. She just stared at Josh, as if she couldn't quite believe it. After a while, she said in a very small voice, "I guess you'd better go, then." Captain Kevin said sorry again, and he and Josh left.

KC looked at Poppy in amazement. "Did that just happen?"

Poppy shook her head in disbelief. "I thought Josh was okay. He and Huxley the dog seemed really cool. We were going to go exploring with them. I just don't get it!"

Tyler shrugged, with a grim look on her face. "I guess some people are just mean," she said. "People are stupid." Then she looked around, as if she remembered that the friends were still there. "I mean, apart from you three." She smiled, just a little bit.

"Hey," said Poppy, having a sudden thought.

"Is the necklace okay?"

Tyler took it out of her pocket. "It's fine. I took it back home with me and fixed it. It's as good as new!" She threw it to Poppy, who caught it and put it safely in her blue backpack.

"Then I suppose we ought to finish cleaning up," said Poppy. She moved the last painting, and sighed to see another patch of purple paint. She was about to clean it up with a cloth, when she noticed something extremely odd.

There was a shoe print in the paint . . . and that shoe print had a lightning bolt through the middle!

"Look!" Poppy called out. "Sam, is this the same shoe as the one in the sand?"

Sam knelt over it. "Yes! Just the same. The AirMax 3000!"

KC came over and looked. "Can it really be the same shoe?"

Poppy's brain felt like it was going at about two hundred miles an hour. "Josh must have left it," she said slowly. "Josh was the only one who could have left a print in the paint!"

"But that means," said Sam, "That Josh must have been the one running away from you on the beach!"

"And that means," said KC, "Josh must have been the one who stole the necklace from I.C.!"

They were all shocked, and suddenly sad - even sadder than when they had found out Josh had messed up the shack. They looked at each other in dismay.

"I thought that when I found out who took the necklace, I'd be happy," said KC. "But this just feels really bad."

Poppy thought desperately. Were they right? Could it really be Josh? He had seemed so happy, playing with his dog, not a necklace-thief. It really didn't seem right. But there was the shoeprint, and Josh had confessed to messing up the shack. There was nothing else to do but finish cleaning and say goodnight to Tyler.

As they walked back home, Poppy tried to fit

the pieces together. "It's just really odd," she said. "Why would anyone steal a necklace and then make a mess like that?"

"I guess Josh isn't so nice after all," said Sam, but he didn't sound very sure about it.

"I don't even want to tell his dad," said KC. "He's in enough trouble already."

"This needs some serious sleep," said Poppy. "Maybe when we wake up tomorrow, we'll know what's going on."

It was hard to get to sleep that night. They didn't even tell Aunt Kathryn what they had worked out. Just before she finally fell asleep, Poppy found herself thinking just one thing: This doesn't feel right. Not right at all.

Chapter 7

Tricks on the Beach

The next morning, Poppy woke up quickly. The sun was shining in through the window onto KC's bed next to hers. KC was still asleep, but Poppy felt wide awake. She felt like her brain had been working all through the night. Once Sam and KC had got up, and they were all having breakfast, she told them what she was thinking.

"I don't think Josh took the necklace," she said firmly.

Sam was so surprised he dropped his toasted bagel on his plate. "But he said he messed up the shack! You heard him."

"I know," said Poppy. "But that doesn't mean the footprint was definitely his. Anyone could have gone into the shack, seen the paint and left the shoe print before Tyler got there! Or maybe he just has the same kind of shoes as the person on the beach. And, anyway," she continued, "I don't think he's the kind of person who would steal a necklace."

The other two nodded. They felt the same way. Even though they had only just met Josh, he didn't seem like the kind of person who would grab other people's property and throw it into the sea for fun.

"We need to talk to Josh and find out the truth," said Poppy.

"At least we can see if he has any AirWave 3000s," KC reminded them. "But he's grounded! There's no way Captain Kevin will let him out to see us!"

"Yes," said Poppy, finishing her cereal, "but I know something we can do. We can look for someone with purple marks on their shoes! If the shoes match, and they've got purple on them, we might have found the person who took the necklace!"

"I don't know," said Sam. "It still seems like Josh is the one who did it. And I don't see how we can keep asking to see the bottom of people's shoes."

"Oh," said KC cheerfully. "You never know!"

"I think I know a way to check for any purple

marks," said Poppy. "Let's go to the beach and I'll show you."

On the beach, the three friends began to talk to any children they saw. "Want to come to a party on the beach?" they asked. Most of the chldren said yes, and then they told them the catch – they could only come if they did a trick!

"Can you do a handstand?" Poppy asked a small boy. As the excited boy tried to get onto his hands, Poppy quickly checked the soles of his shoes. No purple paint.

Sam spotted a chunky girl wearing silver shoes with blue stripes, just like in the picture on the computer. They were AirWave 3000s, all right. "I'll let you come to a party if you can do a kick above your head!" Sam said. The girl kicked high in the air – a bit too high, because she fell over laughing in the sand! Before she could get up, Sam checked the soles of her shoes. No purple marks to be seen.

KC summoned up all her courage, and went up to an older boy wearing a grey hooded top just like the one the person who threw the necklace had been wearing. "Bet you can't stand on one leg for ten seconds," she said. "You can come to our party if you can!"

"That's easy!" said the boy, and lifted one foot off the floor and stood there, wobbling. But KC couldn't quite see the sole of his shoe!

"I mean, you have to lift your leg right up," said KC.

"No fair," said the boy, but he lifted it up higher. There was no paint on his shoe. KC realized she needed to see the other shoe too, just to be sure. "Um . . . now lift up the other leg!"

The boy tried to lift up his other leg and fell over!

"I meant put down the other leg first, then lift it," giggled KC. "Boys!" Anyway, she'd seen both his shoes, and there wasn't a trace of paint on them.

The three friends spent a happy morning getting everyone they met to show them the soles of their shoes. They asked them to do all kinds of crazy tricks, and it was surprising how many people were happy to do them.

"I even got one little girl to do the can-can," laughed Poppy, as they sat on the wall separating the beach and Seaview Street. "Everyone looked pretty silly, but it's okay, because we've made loads of new friends and they're all coming to our party!"

"It's funny," said KC. "If we hadn't secretly been detecting, I would never have been brave enough to ask all those people to do silly tricks. But I'm glad I did!"

"I have to admit, it was funny," said Sam. "Look, there's Aunt Kathryn!"

Aunt Kathryn came jogging along. "Anyone ready for some roller skating?"

"Definitely!" they all said at the same time. "But we don't have our skates with us," Poppy pointed out.

"We'll hire them," said Aunt Kathryn. "I just saw your friend Megan with another girl. They were going roller skating, and I thought you'd like to join them."

Chapter 8

The Owner of the Necklace

Ten minutes later, the three friends were pushing off on their rented roller skates, zooming down Seaview Street. They saw Megan and her friend up ahead, and rushed to catch up. Poppy was in the lead. KC was practicing skating backwards. She was the only one of the three who could do it. Sam was a little way back. He wasn't as good on skates as the girls were.

"Whew!" said Megan, as they finally reached her. "You're all fast! Not as fast as my older brother can go, but he's a fitness trainer, and I think they teach you how to roller skate mega-fast, but he's not here right now, so I guess you're the fastest! This is my friend Isobel. She's staying with me!"

Isobel smiled as she skated along. She was a quiet girl with long pigtails. "When you're friends with Megan,"

thought Poppy, "you have to be quiet because it's hard to get a word in!"

Megan chatted happily as they skated, away from the crush of shoppers and down a quiet road, away from the centre of town. "The bay is pretty great, isn't it?" Poppy asked Isobel. Before she could reply, Megan answered "Oh, yes! Isobel loves the bay. It's her first time here, but she says she's going to come back every year now, isn't that right, Izzy?"

Isobel started to speak. "I used to go . . ."

"She used to go to another beach every year with Dr Carson - that's Isobel's dad - but we're best friends now so I asked her mum if she could come with me and she said yes! We've been walking along the beach every day and having an awesome time," Megan interrupted.

With Megan talking so much as they rolled along, it was a while before Poppy could tell Megan about Tyler's shack. She went through their discovery of Tyler's paintings, and then how Tyler had found everything in the shack ruined. "And then Josh admitted it was him!"

Poppy finished eventually. Isobel and Megan looked surprised. "How mean!" said Isobel.

Something had been nagging at Poppy while she spoke, though. It was something Megan had said. She just couldn't work out what it was. Something about . . ."

"Dr. Carson!" Poppy burst out. Everybody turned to look at her (except Sam, who was trying hard to avoid a tree by the side of the road).

"That's my dad," Isobel said. "What about him?"

"Because," said Poppy slowly, "That means your name is Isobel Carson, right?"

"Yes, that's right," said Isobel, looking puzzled.

Poppy wheeled to a stop and the others did, too. She took off her backpack and felt around inside it. It was a long shot but, just maybe . . .

"I.C.!" said Poppy.

"You see?" asked Megan. "What do you see?"

"No, the initials! I.C.! Isobel, is this yours?" Poppy pulled the rainbow necklace out of her

backpack and showed it to them.

Isobel's eyes widened. "Yes, that's mine! I lost it a few days ago! How did you find it?"

So Poppy told Isobel the story. She told her about the chase, the search, the other person called I.C., the shopkeeper, the whole thing. When she'd finished, she gave the necklace back to Isobel. "We even mended it for you," she said.

Isobel examined the necklace. "That's funny," she said, "Because it wasn't broken when it went missing."

"Put it on, put it on!" said KC, almost jumping up and down with excitement. It was hard to believe they had found the owner of the rainbow necklace! Isobel shyly slipped on the necklace. It looked great, glinting cheerfully in the sun with reds, blues, greens and yellows. They all admired it on her. Everyone except

Sam, who had only just caught up with them, and was trying to keep his balance as he tried to stop too quickly.

"Look out!" he yelled as he sped into the group. Poor Isobel didn't notice. She was too busy fixing the clasp on the necklace, and Sam went rocketing right into her, knocking them both over!

It was hard not to laugh to see a very surprised Isobel on the ground with Sam on top of her, struggling to stand up! Sam and Isobel were both blushing by the time they managed to stand, but in a few minutes even they could see the funny side. It was hard to be embarrassed now that Poppy had been able to give the rainbow necklace back to its rightful owner.

Poppy told Megan and Isobel the rest of the story – how they'd seen the second shoe print in the shack just after Josh had owned up to the mess, and how it matched the one from the runner on the beach. She didn't say that she thought Josh did it, though. It still just didn't seem right. She could see what Megan and

Isobel were thinking, though. They thought it was Josh, too.

They all began to skate back to where Aunt Kathryn was waiting at the beach, only a little slower this time. They were starting to get tired. Roller skating was hard work.

"I forgot Isobel had a necklace like the one you showed me," said Megan, starting to pant. "I didn't know it had gone missing until yesterday. I'll tell you something else, though. On the day Isobel lost her necklace, we were playing with someone. Do I need to tell you who that someone was?" Without waiting for an answer, she carried on. "It was Josh. Josh was the only other person around on the beach that day. It's very suspicious!"

"Uh-oh," thought Poppy. Things didn't look good for Josh.

Chapter 9

Where's Josh?

Aunt Kathryn was very excited the next morning, even though the sky was gloomy and overcast. "Okay, you three!" she said. "We've got lots of fun stuff planned for today! First, we'll hire some wetsuits and bodyboards again, and spend an hour or two on the beach, then we'll head to the pier and see if we can find one of those - "

Poppy interrupted. "Um, Aunt Kathryn?"

"Yes, Poppy?"

"We can't do any of those things."

Aunt Kathryn looked surprised. "What do you mean, Poppy?"

Poppy looked at KC and Sam, and they nodded. The friends had talked, and they had come to a decision.

"We have to talk to Josh," Poppy said. "It's really, really, really important."

"Important enough to forget about bodyboarding this morning?"

Poppy nodded solemnly. "We can't tell you why yet, because it's not fair on Josh if we're wrong. But we need to see him and ask him some questions – as soon as we can."

"That's not going to be easy," said Aunt Kathryn thoughtfully. "He's grounded, and Captain Kevin is pretty strict about this sort of thing. I'm sure Josh is in his bedroom, thinking about what he's done. And I don't think Captain Kevin will let you in."

"We know," sighed KC. "But we have to try."

Aunt Kathryn gave in and told the friends where Josh lived. "But remember, if you can't see him, come back here and we'll go have some fun!"

It didn't take long for the friends to find Josh's house. It was on the edge of the little marina, in sight of Captain Kevin's boat Marlin. They knocked on the door and waited. "Even if Captain Kevin doesn't let us see Josh, and even if he's angry with us, we know we're doing the right thing," said Poppy to KC and Sam. But they all still felt just a bit nervous as they heard someone approach the door and open it.

It was Captain Kevin, but he didn't look angry. He looked worried. "Kids," he said. "Have you seen Josh?"

"We came to speak to him!" said Poppy. "Isn't he inside?"

Captain Kevin ran his fingers through his blond hair. "He's gone!" he said. "He must have ran out of the house after breakfast."

Poppy looked at her friends in confusion. "We really need to speak to him!"

"And I'm really angry with him!" said Captain Kevin. But he didn't look angry. He just looked worried. "It's a mystery where he could have gone to."

"Mystery?" thought Poppy. "We're good at solving mysteries," she said.

Captain Kevin looked rather surprised. Maybe even a little amused.

"Are you?" he said. "Well, do you think you could help find Josh?"

"Definitely," said Poppy. "It's what we do."

KC and Sam agreed.

"Let's go find him!" said KC. She looked ready to run off.

"Wait!" said Poppy, and grabbed KC. "Before we start looking for him, we should talk to Captain Kevin and hunt for clues in Josh's room. That's what real detectives would do."

"You're right," said KC. "Captain Kevin, can we come inside and ask you a few questions?"

Captain Kevin watched as the three friends marched inside. "Oh, well, yes."

They sat around the kitchen table. "Tell us what Josh said before he disappeared," Poppy said.

"He was upset at breakfast," said Captain Kevin, uneasily. "We sort of had a little . . . discussion."

"You mean an argument?" asked Sam.

"I suppose so," said Captain Kevin, looking embarrassed. "He said he'd do all the chores around the house, and clean the boat, if he could go to your party. But I said that until he explained himself, he couldn't go. He just wouldn't tell me why he'd caused all that mess!"

"Did he say anything to you about where he wanted to go?" Poppy asked.

"Not really," said Captain Kevin. "I've tried to think of where he might have gone, but I really don't know. I've been so busy with boat trips lately, I haven't really had much time to spend with Josh."

"Can you remember anything he said this morning that might help us?" asked KC.

Captain Kevin thought hard. "No," he said. "All I remember is that when he left the breakfast table, he was muttering under his breath. Something about falcons, I think. When I asked him what he meant he just shrugged and stormed off. Then when I went to check on him an hour later, he was gone. And he's taken Huxley with him!"

"We need to check his room for clues," said

Poppy. "Is that okay?"

"Of course," said Captain Kevin, "If you think it will help."

"It will help one hundred percent," said Poppy firmly, and they marched upstairs. It was a little strange being in Josh's room without Josh being there. None of them had been there before, and they didn't really know Josh very well yet. It felt like they were barging into someone else's life without permission. Josh's room was messy and filled with all kinds of outdoor equipment: a football, a wetsuit flung onto the floor, a paddle for a canoe. All the posters on the wall were of people skiing, hiking or mountain biking.

"Josh must really like being outside," said Sam. "What's that on the bed?"

It was a piece of paper marked with strange-looking names, and lines connecting them together. "R POOLS, F POINT, LEFT FORK - this doesn't make any sense," said KC.

"Josh loves to explore," said Poppy, thoughtfully. "This must be a kind of map of all the places he's visited. Look, he's marked some directions in between the points. It's just a shame that we don't know what all these names mean. Maybe he's gone to visit one of them."

Sam's eyes were shining. "I know a way to find out," he said. "But we've got to go back to Aunt Kathryn's house. We need the computer!"

Captain Kevin was surprised to see the friends troop downstairs holding the map, and walk straight out the front door.

"Don't worry, Captain Kevin," shouted Poppy as she left. "We've got an important clue. We'll find Josh really soon!"

Chapter 10
The Star Rock

Poppy, KC and Sam ran down the road back to Aunt Kathryn's house. Now that they had left Captain Kevin's house, they could all talk about what they were thinking. Light drops of rain spattered as they hurried down Seaview Street, much emptier now because of the weather.

"Josh has run away because he's worried about the necklace," said KC.

"I've been thinking: he must have seen us give the necklace to Tyler to fix," said Sam. "I think that's why he messed up the shack. He thought the necklace was in there somewhere, and he was looking for it. And now he can't tell anyone in case they figure out that he took the necklace. Then he'll be in even more trouble!"

"I don't know," said Poppy, as they rounded the corner to the house. "Maybe he's just feeling really bad and wanted to get away from everything."

Aunt Kathryn wasn't surprised that they were back so soon. The friends switched on the computer and Sam sat down. Sam was easily the best with computers, and he could find anything he wanted to if he had enough time. He clicked on a button on the screen and started searching. "I need to find a map of the bay," he explained. "Then maybe we can find out all where all these places are."

It didn't take long for Sam to find the map he was looking for. "Can you zoom in?" asked KC.

Sam pressed a button, and the town and the

sea filled the screen.

"We need to see the names of the places, too," said Poppy.

"OK," said Sam. He clicked a button, and the screen showed all the place names of the town.

"Look," said Poppy, her sharp eyes already checking out all the names on the screen. "Falcon Point!" she pointed to the rocky area past the woods outside of the town.

"Captain Kevin said Josh was muttering something about falcons," said KC excitedly.

"And look here!" said Poppy. "F POINT is marked on the map. That must be Falcon Point! That's where Josh must have gone! Well done, Sam! You're a computer genius!"

"It was easy," said Sam, but he looked pleased.

"Aunt Kathryn," asked Poppy, "can we walk up to Falcon Point?"

"Yes," said Aunt Kathryn, "if you're very careful. And don't be long. We've got lots to do when you get back!"

Before long, the three friends were running

down the road back towards Josh's house. "He must have started all his journeys from his house," said Poppy. "So we'll go from there too!" She tried to look at the map as they ran, but it was too difficult to run and read at the same time. "Josh wrote down some things about the journey to Falcon Point," she said. "Maybe they'll help us get there."

Standing outside Josh's house, they looked at the map. "There's a place next to F POINT called THE HIDEAWAY," said Poppy. "That adds up I think. That must be where he is."

Sam started to run up the road. "This way's the quickest," he said, pointing to his print-out of the map they'd seen on the computer screen.

"Wait!" said Poppy, staring closely at Josh's map. "Josh says 'Go by the coast.' We should follow his way."

"Whatever," said Sam. "As long as it gets us there." Instead of taking the straight path up the hill towards Falcon Point, the friends went down to the beach on the other side of the marina. It was much rockier here than on the

sandy beach where they liked to play. There was no sand, only big round pebbles, and the sea splashed them.

"I hope it doesn't rain," said KC, looking at the cloudy sky. At least the raindrops had stopped falling. Nobody wanted to have to find Josh in the middle of a downpour! The crunch of their shoes on the pebbles was the only sound, apart from the splashing waves and the distant seagull cries. The beach curved round and on one side and the rocky cliff started to rise above them as they ran. After a while, Sam stopped them.

"Look!" he said, pointing to his map print-out. "Falcon Point is up there!" They all looked up. The red cliff towered right up above them. Stern rocks jutted from its sides. A few grim little trees hung onto it, almost sticking out into the air. But, mostly, it was bare. "If we'd taken the normal road, we'd be at the top now," grumbled Sam. "But we're stuck down here!"

Poppy looked at Josh's map. "It said he came this way, so there must be a way to get up there," she said. "What's this? 'Look for the star rock'. It's on the line that connects Josh's house on the map to Falcon Point!"

"There must be a star-shaped rock around," said KC. "Let's try to find it."

The three friends rushed to the cliff edge. Sam and KC started examining the rock face, looking for any piece of rock that might look like a star. They gazed up at the cliff that seemed so high above them. Could there really be a way up? After looking at the rock closely, Poppy wandered away, towards the sea.

"Where are you going?" KC called. "Come look."

"That's just what I'm doing," Poppy called back. She walked back across the wide beach until her feet were almost in the water. Then she looked back towards the cliff again. She could see Sam and KC looking very small by the bottom of the cliff. She could see the rocks rise up above them. But if she looked at the whole picture . . .

"Come out here!" she called to Sam and KC, and they came running to the water's edge. "Look up." They looked up and saw what Poppy had seen. Not far from where they had been searching, the whole cliff face formed a massive five-pointed shape. The bottom of two of the 'star's' points touched the ground, and then went sliding up to a central section. Two big arms of rock stuck out high above them, and even higher up, a big triangle of rock formed the fifth point, reaching up almost to the top of the cliff.

"Wow," said Sam. "The star rock."

Poppy marched back towards the star. "Look," she said. "This point touches the ground, and there are sort of rocky steps going up. Let's go!"

Chapter 11

Falcon Point

Poppy began to climb the steps in the cliff, and Sam and KC followed. The steps were steep, but not steep enough to stop them. A big shelf of rock separated the steps from the cliff, so the friends couldn't even see over the side to the beach. Just as they were beginning to feel tired, the steps finished and the path led onto a large, smooth and flat area. As Poppy reached it, she saw that she could see the water again, and if she looked down, she could see the beach. It seemed miles away from them. Looking to her right, Poppy could see the whole of the town laid out below her. She could spot the pier and the beach, and the scattered shops and houses around the town. She even thought that she could make out Captain Kevin's boat, Marlin, as a tiny white glint in the marina. Looking the other way, Poppy could see around the cliff to the forbidding-looking rocks. The beach thinned out and disappeared, and the cliffs jutted straight out of the sea. They had climbed much higher than she thought. She certainly didn't want to go too near the edge of the ledge.

"KC, aren't you scared of heights?" Poppy asked.

"Um, a little bit, sometimes," said KC.

"Okay, well I don't think you should look down," said Poppy.

Sam looked over and saw the view as he got to the top. "We must be in the middle of the star now," he said. "Look - these flat bits in front and behind us are the two, um, sort of arms of the star. I wish someone was down there to take a photo of us up here!"

Poppy helped KC up onto the ledge. KC was trying very hard not to look down.

"It's really windy, isn't it?" KC said, trying to sound calm.

The wind was picking up a little, and they could hear it whistling through the trees above them. Everything felt high and lonely all of a sudden, and Poppy was glad she had KC and

Sam with her. She looked around. There was a path going further up the cliff, just a sandy trail. But now it seemed to be a much more gentle climb away from the beach

"Don't worry, KC," Poppy said, glad there wasn't more cliff-face climbing to be done. "It looks okay from here."

"Don't worry about me," said KC, but Poppy could see KC was holding tightly to the rocks, just in case. "Let's go get Josh!"

The friends marched up the path. There were more trees as they carried on walking, and the path sloped even more gently. Soon, they were walking on flat ground, surrounded by trees. "This must be the wood next to Falcon Point," said Poppy. "We're not far off now."

The trees closed in all around them, and they could feel the odd patter of a raindrop or two fall through the leaves.

"Looks like the rain's here at last," said KC, holding out her hand. "At least we're under cover."

Ahead of them, the little path split into two.

Both ways seemed to lead into the dark woods. "Which way now?" asked Sam. "Does Josh's map say?"

Poppy looked at it again. "It says LEFT FORK. When I saw that earlier in Josh's room, I thought it meant Josh had left a fork here when he was on a picnic!"

KC and Sam grinned, then chuckled, then laughed out loud. So did Poppy. It was just too silly not to!

"What a dumb thing to think! Um, which way is left, again?" asked Sam, and that just sent Poppy and KC into gales of laughter again.

"This way," said Poppy, and they headed down the left path, into the dark trees. It wasn't long before they heard a deep rumble. The sound seemed to be coming from everywhere. "What's that?" wondered KC, zipping up her jacket.

"Thunder, I think," said Poppy. "I hope Josh isn't getting wet!"

The thought of Josh being on his own in a

thunderstorm made them hurry even faster, through the trees and down the thin, little track. To one side, they could still see chinks of sky through the trees, where the cliff edge was. Then without warning, the path opened out into a small clearing. Trees ringed it from three sides, but the other side was open to the sky, facing the bay far below. The friends looked around, surprised.

Poppy looked at the map again. "We're here," she said. "This is where Josh has marked THE HIDEAWAY."

Sam looked around. "I don't see Josh."

"That must be because he's hiding," KC said.

They looked round the clearing. There was a single rock in the middle of it, marked with directions to the other places on the coast. But nobody else seemed to be around. Suddenly, the trees behind them rustled and they heard a bark. They turned in time to see someone drop out of a low tree branch, and land on the ground with a thump.

"Josh!" said Poppy.

Josh stood up and gave them an anxious look. Huxley bounded out from the trees and licked his hand, wagging his tail.

"I can't believe we found you!" said KC happily.

But Josh didn't look very happy at all. "I'm not going back!" he burst out. "And neither is Huxley!"

Without waiting another second, he ran back into the trees, with Huxley bounding after him.

Chapter 12

Josh's Story

"Wait, Josh!" called Poppy, running after him. Sam and KC were right behind her. It was dark in the trees, and it took a little while for Poppy to see Josh picking his way through the undergrowth ahead.

"Josh, come back!" she called. "We only want to talk to you!" "No way!" he called. "You're just like my dad! You want me to sit in my room all day and get bored! I haven't done anything wrong!"

It was hard work trying to scramble through the branches. Even though Josh was just a few steps ahead, Poppy couldn't catch up with him. It felt just like when the person with the necklace had got away, thought Poppy. Was that Josh, too?

"I'm not coming back, so leave me alone," panted Josh. "I just want to – ow!"

Josh tumbled over, and tried to stand up again. "Ouch!" he said, and nearly fell over again.

Poppy tramped quickly through the undergrowth to where Josh was clutching his leg.

"What's happened?" she asked.

Josh looked at her, but he didn't look as angry as he had a minute ago. His face was red and he was breathing fast. Huxley pushed his nose into his hand, and he ruffled Huxley's fur.

"Ow! I think I sprained my ankle." Josh tried to move, but he winced in pain. He grinned at Poppy. "No use trying to run away now, is there?"

Poppy saw a tree stump not far away. "Sit down there," she said. "What do you mean, you've done nothing wrong? What about poor Tyler and her shack?"

Josh didn't look cunning or mischievous, like Poppy thought he might. He just looked sad. "I know," he said. "Poor Tyler."

Sam and KC crashed through the woods and caught up with them. "Why did you go into Tyler's shack and break stuff, Josh? We've been wanting to ask you for days, but we didn't get chance to."

Josh looked at all three of them in turn, as if he was deciding something. He hugged Huxley and let out a long sigh. "I didn't do anything to Tyler's shack," he said. "I didn't even go inside it that morning."

The three friends gazed at him, shocked. "But why did you say you did?" Poppy asked.

"It happened like this," said Josh. "I went downstairs early in the morning, before Dad was awake, to play with Huxley. But Huxley was gone. Sometimes he jumps over the garden fence and runs off, down to the beach. I knew that Dad would be furious when he found out. So I sneaked outside before he was awake. I wanted to find Huxley and bring him home.

"I headed to the beach, but there was no Huxley. Just a set of paw prints in the sand by the beach, leading all the way down to the huts. He likes to sniff around there sometimes." Huxley huffed as if to agree, and Josh patted his head. "I looked around for a while. The sun had only just come up and there was nobody else around. I wandered around the shacks, calling to Huxley.

I found him outside Tyler's shack. The door was open and I could see that there was a horrible mess inside. I looked at Huxley. He had purple paint all down one side of him, sticking to his fur! I was so angry at him. I shouted at him and he looked very sorry.

"Huxley had never made a mess like that before. But I knew he must have gone into the shack and pulled everything apart. He didn't know he was being bad. If Dad found out,  Huxley would get taken away or locked up forever. No more walks on the beach - no more games - nothing." Josh looked sad, holding on to Huxley as if someone would come to take him away that minute.

"I knew I had to get Huxley away from there," Josh went on. "I took Huxley down to the beach and washed off as much of the paint as I could. I still think he's got some on his coat, but no one has seen it. Then we went home."

"What happened next?" said KC, fascinated.

"We had no idea all this happened!"

"When I got in, Dad wasn't even up yet. I let Huxley out the back door, and went back up to my bedroom. The trouble was, Dad got up just as I was coming upstairs. I didn't realize that I still had some purple paint on me. Dad was furious. He asked me what I'd been doing, going out and messing up my clothes before breakfast. At first I stayed quiet, but later I realised that Dad would hear about the shack and work it out for himself. So, at lunch, I lied and told him that I'd made a mess of Tyler's shack. He marched me down there and, well, you know the rest," Josh finished.

"So you lied about it just to protect Huxley?" Poppy asked. Josh nodded. He still wasn't letting Huxley go. The rain spattered around them through the trees as they stood there, not knowing what to say. It seemed strange to lie about doing something so bad, just to protect a dog.

"It was brave. I think you're brave," said Sam. "Trying to save Huxley like that."

"Me too!" said KC. "Imagine everyone thinking you've done something so bad, just to keep Huxley safe."

Josh smiled a little. "It was okay at first, being in the house all day," he said. "But this morning I just felt I was going to burst! Dad was talking about stopping my allowance and not letting me go to your party, and I just had to get out!"

Suddenly, Poppy remembered something very important. "Josh," she asked, "do you have a pair of AirMax 3000s?"

"Those super-cool shoes?" said Josh, looking surprised. "I wish! I've just got these old ones." He pointed at his tattered sneakers. "I wear them all the time. Why?"

"Because," said Poppy, "someone who wore those shoes was in the shack. They left a footprint in the paint."

"You mean," said Josh, thoughtfully, "a person might have made that mess?"

Poppy nodded.

"You mean," Josh continued, "someone who wasn't Huxley?"

Poppy nodded again.

"You mean," said Josh, "it wasn't Huxley at

all?" His eyes were wide and he began to grin.

"Huxley!" he yelled. "You're innocent! I knew you didn't do it! I knew! I knew! Ouch!" Josh yelled as he tried to stand up to do a dance and almost fell over on his twisted ankle. He didn't seem to mind, though. He picked up Huxley's front paws and made him dance, then hugged him close. Poppy, KC and Sam felt just as happy. They couldn't help petting Huxley too. The big dog was overjoyed at all the attention. He barked happily, jumped up at Josh and let his mouth hang open in the biggest doggy grin ever!

"We have to go tell my Dad," Josh said when they'd calmed down. "Then he won't be angry with me any more. And you can tell him that you know that Huxley didn't do it. Right?"

"Right," Poppy said, as she thought about the way back, down the cliff. "But how are we going to get you back? You can't go down steps with an ankle like that."

Josh's ankle looked red and sore. He tried to stand up again and walk, but he was only able to hobble slowly.

"It's okay," Josh said. "I know a way back through the woods and into town. If only I had my map with me. It's got places marked on it that only I can read."

Poppy gave Josh his map. He took it, surprised.

"It's how we found you," she said, and explained about their journey to Falcon Point.

"Wow," said Josh, his eyes shining. "You three really are detectives!"

The three friends felt very proud, and they all smiled. The journey to Falcon Point had definitely been worth it.

Looking at his map, Josh led them slowly through the woods, singing at the top of his voice all the way. "I'm innocent! Huxley is innocent! We're saved!"

It wasn't long before they found the road and walked back down into town. The rain was stopping, and the sun was shining again. As they reached the marina and Josh's house, Sam tapped Poppy on the shoulder. "If Josh didn't leave the footprints, take the necklace or trash the shack - then who did?"

"It's still a mystery," said Poppy. "But look at everything we've found out today. I'm sure we can find out."

When Captain Kevin opened the door to Josh, he grabbed him and gave him a huge hug. At first, he didn't even hear Josh trying to explain everything all at once. Captain Kevin was just glad that Josh was safe.

After they had told Captain Kevin the whole story, and Josh and his dad were friends again, the friends headed home. All three felt very tired. What a day! Aunt Kathryn was waiting for them. "I was worried you were caught in the thunderstorm," she said. "Let's hope the weather is better tomorrow. For your party, I mean."

"Oh!" cried Poppy. "The party!"

Sam and KC looked just as surprised as she was. Aunt Kathryn looked at them and laughed. "Don't tell me you forgot about it?"

Poppy grinned with anticipation. "Well, maybe just for a while," she said.

Chapter 13

Beach Party

But the next day was as hot and sunny. Poppy, KC and Sam didn't have much time to think about the rainbow necklace that morning. They were too busy helping Aunt Kathryn to prepare for the party. Poppy and Aunt Kathryn were in the kitchen, baking cupcakes. They made chocolate, Poppy's favourite, peanut butter, Sam's favourite and vanilla, KC's favourite. Soon, they had a mountain of cakes, which they wrapped up and loaded into the back of Aunt Kathryn's car. Sam sat at the computer, downloading lots of great ideas for party games they could play on the beach.

KC was with Tyler, at her shack. They were working on a top-secret project that they didn't want to tell anyone about. KC was especially good at keeping secrets. You have to be good at keeping secrets if you won't even tell anyone what the letters in your name stand for!

When Aunt Kathryn had first told them about the party, Poppy thought she would be waiting for it impatiently all week. But so much had happened. Helping Tyler, returning the necklace and, now, finding all about Josh and Huxley. Poppy hadn't had time to think about the party at all! And now it was party time.

Aunt Kathryn drove them all to the beach in her little car, even though it was just at the end of the street. It was the easiest way to carry everything they needed. While Aunt Kathryn set up the barbecue at the top of the beach, Poppy, KC and Sam put up Aunt Kathryn's big volleyball net. Even though the beach was very popular today, there was still a lot of room to play and run around. They sat on the big cooler to catch their breath.

"I almost forgot that it's our last day on the beach before Mum and Dad come to take us back home," said Poppy. "Somehow, I really thought we'd find out who took the rainbow necklace before we went home."

"Do we have to go home?" asked Sam.

"Poppy," said KC nervously, "What if nobody comes to our party?"

But she needn't have worried. Before they had finished setting up, people were already running up to join them. Soon, everyone was splashing in the water or playing tag in the sand. Aunt Kathryn talked to the other grown-ups and put some food on the barbecue. It sizzled and smoked and filled the air with delicious smells.

Soon, Isobel and Megan turned up. "We wouldn't have missed your party for anything,"

said Megan. "Not for a huge heap of gold or a pony or, or a hundred rainbow necklaces!" Isobel nodded in agreement. Poppy was delighted to see that Isobel had the rainbow necklace on. It looked so pretty, shining in the sun.

Josh arrived, looking very happy. He'd brought Huxley with him, and everyone gave Huxley pats and hugs.

"How's your ankle, Josh?" asked Poppy.

"Much better!" said Josh. "I can't run very far today, but I don't need to. Huxley will do it for me. Watch!"

Josh took out a Frisbee and threw it down the beach. "Catch, Huxley!" he yelled. Huxley chased it, jumped up and caught the Frisbee in his mouth. Everyone whooped and cheered, and Huxley looked extremely pleased.

"You know, Huxley was sad when I was stuck indoors," said Josh to Poppy. "But now he's as happy as ever – thanks to you."

Tyler showed up a little later, carrying a big covered canvas. She wouldn't show anyone what was underneath it, but Poppy saw her winking at KC. It must be their secret project, Poppy thought. Instead of joining everyone, Tyler sat on a big rock, watching.

"Come on, Tyler!" called KC.

"I'm not playing those children's games," mumbled Tyler.

The three friends disagreed, and pulled Tyler to her feet. In a moment or two, Tyler was running about and laughing as much as any of them.

Poppy, Tyler, Sam and Josh started playing a game of volleyball - boys versus girls. Poppy and Tyler were in the lead, and Poppy was about to slap the ball over the net. But as she looked down, something caught her eye. She couldn't work out what had made her stop. Something in the sand, something she'd seen before. She paused, and the ball went right over her head.

"Nice try, Poppy!" laughed Sam. "Are you taking a nap over there?"

Poppy didn't even notice. She got down on her

hands and knees and looked at the sand. There was some kind of pattern in it. It didn't take her long to spot it. A shoeprint in the 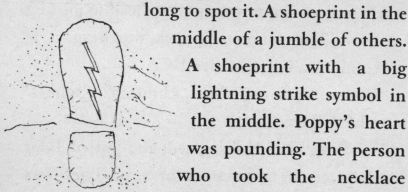 middle of a jumble of others. A shoeprint with a big lightning strike symbol in the middle. Poppy's heart was pounding. The person who took the necklace couldn't be here. Or could they? Poppy ran from the game.

"Back soon!" she yelled. She remembered Sam showing her a picture of the AirMax 3000s. They were a silvery colour with blue stripes. She looked around at everyone playing happily in the sun. Who had Airmax 3000s on? People started laughing at her as she ran around the party area with her head ducked down, trying to look at everyone's shoes. Nobody seemed to have AirMax 3000s on! Poppy rushed over to KC, who was giggling as she tried to bury Isobel in the sand.

"Quick, KC! Has anyone left the party?"

"I don't think so," said KC, looking puzzled. "Everyone's here. I guess Megan went to go to the bathroom a few minutes ago, but that's it.

"Poppy leaned over and started whispering in KC's ear.

Chapter 14
Solved!

When Megan came back a couple of minutes later, Poppy, Sam and KC were sitting away from everyone else, paddling their toes in the warm water. If Megan had looked hard at them, she might have seen that they looked like they had something on their minds. As if they were trying to hide something, even. But Megan didn't look.

"Hey, Megan!" Poppy called. "Come take off your shoes and paddle!"

"Oh, okay," said Megan. "I'm pretty good at paddling, even though I know it's not like a competition where you can be better than anyone else, but still I'm pretty good." She sat down and started taking off her shoes. Poppy looked closely at those shoes. Silver, with blue stripes! AirMax 3000s!

Sam and KC got out of the water and sat down next to Megan.

"What are you doing?" Megan asked,

nervously. "Aren't we going in the water?"

She took off her shoes and put them down in the sand. Quick as a flash, Sam grabbed one and KC grabbed the other. They held them up to Poppy and both said, "Purple paint!"

Poppy could see the purple stain all over one sole, and splashes of purple all over the side of the other shoe.

Megan looked horrified. For once, she was lost for words. She got up as if she was about to run - and then burst into tears.

"It's true!" she sobbed. "It's all me! It's all my fault! I took the rainbow necklace! I ruined Tyler's shack! I did it all! Oh, I'm a terrible, terrible person!"

It was a good thing for Megan that they were sitting away from everyone else, down by the water. Nobody else could hear her, or see she was crying. Poppy looked at Megan in dismay.

"But Megan, you're Isobel's best friend! Why did you do it?"

Megan sniffed and looked at Poppy. "I couldn't tell anyone," she said. "I'm so bad! I should be grounded for years, or until I'm old, or maybe forever!"

To Poppy's surprise, KC put her arm around Megan. "Tell us what happened," she said softly. And Megan did.

"It all started when Isobel got her beautiful new necklace. We'd just got here and I was so excited to show her around. We went everywhere - in the rock pools, down the beach, up to the cliffs. It was just amazing. I'd never had a best friend before, you see." Megan looked at KC and Poppy. "It's different for you two. You do everything together. It's never been like that for me! Anyway, Isobel had some money from her mother. She said she could spend it on anything she wanted. She went into a shop in town, and when she came out she had a beautiful necklace, with stones that were all the colours of the rainbow. I asked if I could try it on, but she was too happy wearing it to even notice. And I didn't have anything. She had lots and lots of beautiful things like that. It wasn't fair. The next day, when we were on the beach playing with Josh, she put the necklace in her bag when we went swimming. I just wanted to try it on, to wear it for a while. Before I knew it, my hand had gone into Isobel's bag and grabbed the necklace. But I didn't put it on. I put it in my bag. I don't know why!" Megan looked very upset.

"When Isobel came back, she didn't notice that the necklace was missing. Why would she? She has so many of them. So I took it home with me. I was so scared that she would realise it was gone, but she never did. The next day, I was too afraid to speak to Isobel. I left her playing with Josh, on the beach and went for a walking by myself. I just wanted to wear the necklace for a little while. I thought I could slip it back in her bag when she wasn't looking. But then something awful happened. I tripped and fell onto a rock. I wasn't hurt, but when I looked at the necklace, I saw that I'd broken it! The chain was snapped. I was going to be in terrible trouble now. There was no way I could put it back. I'd have to see the look on Isobel's face when she found it was broken. I was suddenly so, so worried. I just wanted to get rid of the necklace, some way, any way. I was a thief and a bad friend and I didn't want to see it any more. So without thinking I grabbed the necklace and threw it as far as I could, far out into the water. I thought that would be the end of it. Maybe Isobel would see that the necklace was missing and be very sad - but she'd never know it was me. Except, the necklace landed in the water next to you, Poppy. I was so upset, I didn't even see you and KC swimming there. You grabbed the necklace out of the water before it sank. When you started calling out and splashing towards me, I panicked, pulled my hood up so you wouldn't see who I was, and ran off as fast as I could go." Megan ran out of breath and words at the same time, and looked down at the sand.

"So it was you all along," said Sam. "You were the runner on the beach."

Megan nodded and sniffed again. "I couldn't believe it when I heard your voice calling after me, Poppy. I didn't even know you were staying here! I knew if you saw me, you would ask me all kinds of questions. So I ran faster than I've ever run in my life. I raced across the rock pools and up towards Seaview Street. If it hadn't been for those shoes . . . " Megan pointed to the AirMax 3000s, ". . . I would never have got away."

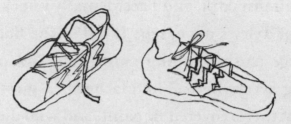

"But if it wasn't for those shoes," said Poppy softly, "We wouldn't have found you."

"There's one thing I don't get," said KC. "What about the shack? How come you made a mess in there?"

"Oh, that!" said Megan. "As if things weren't bad enough! I knew that Poppy had the necklace. I just wanted to get it back into Isobel's bag without anyone finding out about me. I followed you three to the shack and looked through the window. I saw you handing the necklace over to Tyler. I thought you were giving it to her."

Poppy shook her head.

"I know, I know," said Megan. "Tyler was just fixing it for you. I thought she was going to keep it in the shed. So I came back early the next morning when she wasn't there and crept inside the shack. I had to find the necklace! But it was still almost dark, and I accidentally knocked over one of Tyler's big easels. It fell to the floor with a huge crash, sending paint pots and pictures flying everywhere. The place was a mess! I ran out of there, covered in paint, and who did I see? Huxley the dog, coming across the sand! I saw a way to pin the blame on someone else. I didn't want people to think I was a vandal as well as a thief! I smeared paint on Huxley's side so it would look as if he had made the mess. Then I ran back home and got changed before anyone saw me."

"Oh, Megan," said Poppy. "That was a pretty bad thing to do."

"I know, I know. Poppy, you're so much better than me," said Megan, sadly. "You got the necklace fixed, found out it belonged to Isobel and gave it back to her. I was so relieved! I didn't think anyone would ever know what I did. But I was so excited about your party, I forgot to take the stupid, stupid paint off my shoes."

"What are you going to do now?" asked Sam.

Megan stood up sadly. "I don't know," she said. "If Isobel finds out that I borrowed her necklace without asking, she'll never want me to be friends again."

"Don't worry," said Poppy. "Isobel won't feel that way. I'm sure she'll understand."

For the first time, Megan looked hopeful. "You really think so?"

"I know so," said Poppy. "But you have to tell her the truth!"

Megan nodded, swallowed and looked over at where Isobel was playing happily. Looking determined, she walked over and began to speak with her. Poppy, KC and Sam were too far away to hear what they were saying. But they could see the expressions on their faces.

At first, Isobel looked very surprised.

Then, as Megan continued to talk, Isobel at first looked angry then her face softened. She held Megan's hand. When Megan finished talking, Megan and Isobel gave each other a big hug.

"I think they're still friends," said KC.

Megan looked over towards Poppy, KC and Sam. She still looked sad, but she looked relieved as well. She turned and gave the friends a thumbs-up sign. Then Megan and Isobel wandered off up the beach together, still talking, and still holding hands.

"I knew it!" said Poppy. "Telling Isobel the truth was the best thing Megan could do."

She looked at KC, who was smiling at her. As Poppy watched, KC shouted out loud. "Woo-hoo!"

Sam and Poppy looked at KC in surprise. "What did you do that for?" asked Sam. "That's not a very KC thing to do."

KC laughed. "Because you did it, Poppy! You really did it! You finally solved the mystery of the rainbow necklace!"

Poppy smiled and gave them both a hug. "I didn't do it, guys. We did!"

But that wasn't quite the end of the story. When they returned to the party, KC and Tyler had one last surprise for everyone. They stood next to the covered object that Tyler had brought from the shack and, together, they pulled off the sheet that covered it.

Underneath was a big canvas. And on the canvas was a painting of all the people they'd met this vacation.

Josh was on there, smiling, and Huxley was jumping up at him with his big grin on his face. Captain Kevin stood next to them, his hand proudly on Josh's shoulder. Megan and Isobel were arm in arm, and Isobel even had the rainbow necklace around her neck. In the middle of the painting, next to Aunt Kathryn, stood Tyler with Poppy, KC and Sam.

Poppy and everyone else was overjoyed. They all cheered and clapped. Tyler and KC both looked very embarrassed. Tyler pointed to a blank patch of wall on a building bordering the beach. "I've asked permission, and I'm going to turn it into a mural on that wall," said Tyler, blushing a little at all the attention. "That way, we can all remember this summer."

Aunt Kathryn put some music on her portable player, and it wasn't long before everyone was dancing. Poppy, KC and Sam were having so much fun, they managed to forget that it was the last afternoon they'd be able to spend on the beach.

In the middle of the party, Aunt Kathryn's phone rang. "Poppy! Sam!" she called out, "It's your parents!"

Sam and Poppy came running up as Aunt Kathryn spoke on the phone. "Oh, that's annoying!" she said. "No, that's fine. I'm sure they'll cope." She said goodbye and flipped her phone closed.

"Are they coming to pick us up tonight?" asked Sam. "I thought we had one last night here."

"Looks like your parents are stuck at an

airport on the other side of the country," said Aunt Kathryn, trying to look serious. "They'll be back soon, but I'm afraid it means... you're going to have to stay with me for one more day."

Poppy and Sam cheered. "Aunt Kathryn," said Poppy, "This really is the best summer ever. Thanks so much for helping us have such a great time!"

Aunt Kathryn smiled at them. "From what I've seen today," she said, "It looks like you three have been the ones helping people out. And now, aren't you forgetting something?"

"What do you mean?" said Poppy. "We've given the necklace back and we've found the person who took it. What's left?"

"Only one thing, said Aunt Kathryn. "You need to solve the mystery of why you haven't eaten all the food yet!"

Poppy laughed as she ran to pile her plate high. "Don't worry. We're on the case!"

If you've enjoyed meeting Poppy, KC and Sam, you can try one of these other exciting books in the *Three Together* series.